Merry Christmas, Timothy!

love,

Nonnie
& Granpa

Dec. 25, 2008

Stories in This Book

Richard Scarry's
Animal Nursery Tales

A GOLDEN BOOK • NEW YORK

www.goldenbooks.com
www.randomhouse.com/kids

Library of Congress Cataloging-in-Publication Data

Scarry, Richard.
    Richard Scarry's animal nursery tales.— 1st Random House ed.
        p. cm.
    ISBN-13: 978-0-375-83791-3   ISBN-10: 0-375-83791-4
    [1. Folklore. 2. Fairy tales.] I. Title: Animal nursery tales. II. Title.
PZ8.1.S28Ri 2006
398.2–dc22

2006002064

PRINTED IN SINGAPORE   10 9 8 7 6 5 4 3 2 1

First Random House Edition 2006

LITTLE RED RIDING HOOD

Once upon a time, there was a little girl. She was called Little
Red Riding Hood because she always wore a red cape with a hood.

Little Red Riding Hood lived with her mother in a little house on
the edge of a deep, dark forest.

One day, her mother said to her, "Your grandmother is not feeling
well. I want you to take her some goodies."

She gave a basket of cookies and cakes to Little Red Riding Hood
and said, "Don't dawdle along the way. I want you home before dark."

Little Red Riding Hood put on her red cape
with the hood and set out through the woods to
visit her grandmother.

As she was skipping along the path, a wolf suddenly stepped out from behind a tree. Little Red Riding Hood was so frightened, she almost dropped her basket.

But the wolf smiled and said in his sweetest gruff voice, "Where are you going, little miss?"

"I am taking some goodies to my sick grandmother," answered Little Red Riding Hood.

"And where does your grandmother live?" asked the wolf politely.

"In a little white cottage in the middle of the forest," replied Little Red Riding Hood.

"Ah," said the wolf, "I know that house."

"I hope your grandmother will be feeling better soon," he called, slinking back behind the trees.

Little Red Riding Hood went on her way.

When Little Red Riding Hood was out of sight, the crafty wolf ran with all his might, by a shortcut, to Grandmother's house. He wanted to get there first.

He arrived breathless at Grandmother's house and knocked on the door.

"Who is there?" called Grandmother.

"It is I, Little Red Riding Hood," said the wolf, trying to make his rough voice sound soft.

"Just pull the latch string and come in, my dear," said Grandmother.

The wolf came in.

He leaped at Grandmother and swallowed her whole!

Then that crafty fellow put on a nightdress and a nightcap and climbed into bed to wait for Little Red Riding Hood.

"She will think I am her grandmother," he chuckled to himself.

In a minute, there was a knock at the door.
"Who is it?" called the wolf, trying to sound like Grandmother.
"It is I, Little Red Riding Hood," answered the little girl.
"Just pull the latch string and come in, my dear," said the wolf.
Little Red Riding Hood came in and put her basket down.

"Come closer, my dear," said the wolf.
"Why, Grandma, what big ears you have!" said Little Red Riding Hood.
"All the better to hear you with, my dear," said the wolf in his best grandmother voice.

"And Grandma, what big eyes you have!" the little girl said.
"All the better to see you with, my dear," said the wolf.

9

"And Grandma," said Little Red Riding Hood, "what big teeth you have!"

"All the better to EAT you with, my dear!" howled the wicked wolf.

Then he leaped out of bed and tried to grab Little Red Riding Hood.

But Little Red Riding Hood was too quick for him. She ran out the door screaming for help.

A sturdy woodchopper who was nearby rushed after the wolf and conked him on the head. The wolf fell dead.

Then the woodchopper noticed that something was
moving around inside the wolf.

He cut the wolf open, and out popped Grandmother.
She was all right, but a little bit upset by her experience.
It was a good thing the wolf was so greedy that he
had swallowed her whole!

The woodchopper carried Grandmother
back to her bed. Then they all had a snack from
Little Red Riding Hood's basket of goodies.

Grandmother thanked the woodchopper
for saving their lives, and kissed Little
Red Riding Hood goodbye.

Then the kindly woodchopper took
Little Red Riding Hood home—just
in time for her supper.

11

THE GINGERBREAD MAN

Once upon a time, a little old woman and a little old man lived in a little old house.

One day, the little old woman decided to make a gingerbread man.

She cut him out of dough and put him in the oven to bake.

After a while, the little old woman said to herself, "That gingerbread man must be ready by now."

She went to the oven door and opened it. Up jumped the gingerbread man, and away he ran, out the front door.

As he ran, he shouted,
"Run, run as fast as you can.
You can't catch me,
I'm the gingerbread man!"

The little old woman ran after the gingerbread man, but she couldn't catch him.

He ran past the little old man, who was working in his garden.
"Run, run as fast as you can.
You can't catch me,
I'm the gingerbread man!
I've run away from a little old woman,
and I can run from you, I can!"

The little old man ran, but he couldn't catch the gingerbread man.

The gingerbread man came to a field of mowers. He called out as he went by,
"I've run away from a little old woman,
and a little old man,
and I can run from you, I can!"

13

The mowers ran after him . . .

. . . but they couldn't catch him.

The gingerbread man ran on until he came to a cow.

"Run, run as fast as you can.
You can't catch me,
I'm the gingerbread man!
I've run away from a little old woman,
a little old man,
and a field full of mowers,
and I can run from you, I can!"

14

The cow ran . . .

. . . but she couldn't catch him.

He ran between two picnicking bears.
"I've run away from a little old woman,
and a little old man,
a field full of mowers,
and a cow,
and I can run from you, I can!"

The bears jumped up
and ran after him.

They ran,

and ran,

but they couldn't catch
that gingerbread man.

17

Soon the gingerbread man came to a fox
lying by the side of a river, and he shouted,

"Run, run, as fast as you can.
You can't catch me,
I'm the gingerbread man!
I've run away from a little old woman,
and a little old man,
a field full of mowers,
a cow,
and two picnicking bears,
and I can run from you, I can!"

But the sly fox just laughed and said,
"If you don't get across this river quickly,
you will surely get caught. If you hop on
my tail, I will carry you across."

The gingerbread man saw that he had no time
to lose, so he quickly hopped onto the fox's tail.

"Oh!" said the fox. "The water's getting
deeper. Climb up on my back so you won't
get wet."
And the gingerbread man did.

"Look out!" said the fox. "The water's even
deeper. Climb up on my head so you won't
get wet."

And the gingerbread man did.

"It's too deep! It's too deep!" cried the fox. "Climb up on my nose so you won't get wet!"

And the gingerbread man did.

Then, with a flick of his head, the fox tossed the gingerbread man into his mouth. His jaws snapped shut . . .

. . . and that was the end
of the gingerbread man!

THE THREE LITTLE PIGS

Once upon a time, there were three little pigs. When they were old enough, they left their home to seek their fortunes.

Mother Pig was very sad to see them leave.

The first little pig met a farmer with a load of straw.

"Please, sir," he said, "will you give me some straw to build a house?"

The farmer gave the first little pig some straw.

And the little pig built
a house of straw.

Along came a wicked wolf and knocked
on the door.

"Little pig, little pig, let me come in,"
said the wolf.

But the little pig answered, "No, no!
Not by the hair of my chinny-chin-chin."

"Then I'll huff and I'll puff and I'll blow
your house in," said the wolf.

And he huffed and he puffed
and he blew the house in,
and he ate the little pig up.

23

The second little pig met a woodcutter with a bundle of sticks.

"Please, sir," he asked, "may I have some sticks to build a house?"

The woodcutter gave him some sticks, and the second little pig built his house of sticks.

Then along came the wolf, who said, "Little pig, little pig, let me come in."

"No, no! Not by the hair of my chinny-chin-chin," answered the second little pig.

"Then I'll huff and I'll puff and I'll blow your house in," said the wolf.

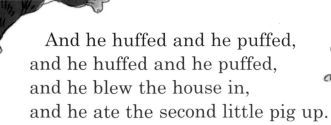

And he huffed and he puffed, and he huffed and he puffed, and he blew the house in, and he ate the second little pig up.

The third little pig met a bricklayer with a load of bricks.

"Please, sir," he asked, "may I have some bricks to build a house?"

The bricklayer gave him some bricks, and the third little pig built his house of bricks.

Then along came the wolf, who said, "Little pig, little pig, let me come in."

And the third little pig answered, "No, no! Not by the hair of my chinny-chin-chin."

"Then I'll huff and I'll puff and I'll blow your house in," said the wolf. So the wolf huffed and he puffed and he huffed and he puffed.

He huffed and he puffed until he could
huff and puff no more.
But he couldn't blow the little house in.

"I must think of a trick to get that little
pig out of his house," the crafty wolf said
to himself.

After thinking for a while, he said, "Little pig,
I know of a garden where there are some tasty
turnips. Will you join me at seven o'clock tomorrow
morning and we will go get some?"
"Where are they?" asked the little pig.
"Down in Misty Meadows," said the wolf.
The little pig agreed to go.

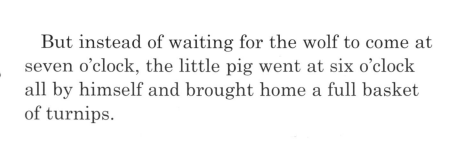

But instead of waiting for the wolf to come at
seven o'clock, the little pig went at six o'clock
all by himself and brought home a full basket
of turnips.

When the wolf came at seven o'clock, he asked the little pig if he was ready to go.

"Why, I have been there already," said the little pig, "and I have brought home a full basket of turnips for dinner."

The wolf was very angry at this, but he pretended not to be.

He thought of another trick.

"Little pig, I know where there is a nice apple tree," he said.

"Where?" asked the little pig.

"Over at Windy Hill," said the wolf. "I will come for you at six o'clock tomorrow morning and we will go together to pick some juicy apples."

Well, the little pig got up at five o'clock the next morning and went to the apple tree, hoping to get back home before the wolf came.

But it took him a long time to get there.

He was still up in the tree when he saw the wolf coming.

He was very frightened.

27

The wolf stopped under the tree and said, "Little pig, you got here before me. Are they nice apples?"

"Yes," said the little pig. "I will throw one down for you to taste."

But he threw it so far that when the wolf ran to catch it, the little pig climbed down and ran home.

The next day, the wolf came to the little pig's house again. "Little pig, there is a fair at Shanklin this afternoon. Will you go with me?" he asked.

"Oh, yes," said the little pig. "When shall I meet you?"

"At three o'clock," said the wolf.

So the little pig, as usual, went earlier. At the fair, he bought a butter churn to make butter in.

As the little pig was going home with it, he saw
the wolf coming up the road. He didn't know
what to do.

He decided to climb
into the churn to hide.

But the churn tipped over and rolled
down the hill.
    The wolf was so frightened by it that he
ran away home without going to the fair
to find the little pig.

Now, when the wolf found out that the little pig had been inside the churn, he was furious.

He went to the little pig's house.

"Little pig, little pig," he called, "you got away from me at Misty Meadows, Windy Hill, and the Shanklin Fair, but you can't get away from me now. I am coming down the chimney to eat you up!"

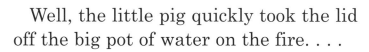

Well, the little pig quickly took the lid off the big pot of water on the fire. . . .

SPLASH! Into the boiling water fell the wolf!

The wolf jumped up and ran howling out the door, never to return to the little brick house, where the little pig lived happily ever after.

GOLDILOCKS AND THE THREE BEARS

Once upon a time, there were three bears who lived in a little house in the woods.

Father Bear was a great big bear.

Mother Bear was a medium-sized bear.

And Baby Bear was a wee tiny bear.

One day, Mother Bear made hot porridge for breakfast.

She poured it into their bowls, and they all went for a walk in the woods while it cooled.

While they were gone, a little girl named Goldilocks came to their house.

She looked in the door and didn't see anyone there, so in she went. Now, that was not right. She should have waited for someone to come home.

Well, Goldilocks saw porridge on the table and suddenly felt very hungry.

She tasted the porridge in Father Bear's great big bowl. But that was too hot!

She tasted the porridge in Mother Bear's medium-sized bowl. But that was too cold!

Then she tasted the porridge in Baby Bear's wee tiny bowl. And that was just right! So she ate it all up.

Then she decided to sit down for a rest.
She sat in Father Bear's great big chair.
But that was too high!

She sat in Mother Bear's
medium-sized chair.
But that was too wide!

Then she sat in Baby Bear's
wee tiny chair.
And that was neither too high
nor too wide. It was just right!

But the wee tiny chair was
not strong enough, and it broke
all to pieces.

Then Goldilocks felt a little sleepy, so she decided to go upstairs and take a nap.

First she lay down in Father Bear's great big bed.
But that was too hard!

Then she lay down in Mother Bear's medium-sized bed.
But that was too soft!

Then she lay down in Baby Bear's wee tiny bed.
And that was just right!
She snuggled under the covers and soon was fast asleep.

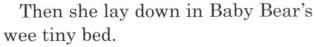

Then the Bears came back from their walk.

Father Bear saw a spoon in his great big porridge bowl.

"Someone has been tasting my porridge," said Father Bear in his deep gruff voice.

Mother Bear saw a spoon in her medium-sized porridge bowl.

"Someone has been tasting *my* porridge," she said in her medium-sized voice.

"Someone has been tasting my porridge," said Baby Bear in his wee tiny voice, "and has eaten it all up!"

Then Father Bear noticed that the cushion was not straight on his great big chair.

"Someone has been sitting in my chair," he roared in his deep gruff voice.

Mother Bear noticed that the cushions on her medium-sized chair were all mussed, too.

"Someone has been sitting in *my* chair," she said in her medium-sized voice.

"And someone has been sitting in my chair, and has broken it all to pieces," said Baby Bear in his wee tiny voice.

Then the three bears went upstairs to see what they would find there.

"Someone has been sleeping in my bed," said Father Bear in his deep gruff voice.

"Someone has been sleeping in *my* bed," said Mother Bear in her medium-sized voice.

"Someone has been sleeping in my bed," said Baby Bear in his wee tiny voice, "and here she is!"

When Goldilocks heard Baby Bear's wee tiny voice, she
awakened in a fright. She jumped up out of the wee tiny
bed, scrambled down the stairs, and ran out of the house.
And she didn't stop running until she got home.

And she never again went
to the house of the Three Bears.

THE WOLF AND THE KIDS

Once upon a time, a mother goat and her seven
little kids lived in a cozy house near a deep
forest. And in that forest lived a wicked wolf.

One day, Mother Goat had to go shopping. She
called her children to her and warned them,
"Lock the door and do not open it to anyone
while I am gone, for it might be the wicked wolf,
who will want to eat you up."

The seven kids promised not to open the door
to anyone, and Mother Goat went on her way.

Shortly after she left, there was a knocking at the door.

"Let me in, my dear children," a voice said. "It is your mother, and I have brought something for each of you. Open the door and let me in."

The seven kids were ready to open the door when they saw a black paw on the windowsill.

"You are not our mother!" they cried. "Our mother's paw is white, and yours is black. You are the wicked wolf! Go away!"

So the wicked wolf went to the baker and said, "Cover my paws with white flour or I will eat you up."

The poor baker was very frightened, so he did as he was told.

The wolf went back to the cozy house near the forest and put his white paw on the windowsill.

"Open the door, my dear children," he said. "It's your mother, and I have brought something for each of you."

The seven kids saw the white paw. "It's Mother!" they cried, and they opened the door.

In bounded the wicked wolf!

The kids ran to hide.

The first ran under the table.

The second sprang into bed.

The third hid in a laundry basket.

The fourth jumped into a barrel.

The fifth climbed into a cupboard.

The sixth crawled under a washtub.

And the seventh and youngest got into the grandfather clock.

But the wolf found them and popped them into his sack—all but the youngest, who was in the grandfather clock. Then that wicked wolf started back home through the forest.

The sack was so heavy that he soon had to stop and lie down for a rest. And he dozed off, dreaming of the fine supper he would have.

When Mother Goat arrived home, everything was topsy-turvy.

And her children were nowhere to be found! Then she heard a noise in the clock.

Out jumped the youngest kid, who told his mother how the wolf had tricked them.

Mother Goat set out to find the wolf, and soon she came upon him snoring under a tree. She saw something moving in the sack.

The rope around the sack was so tight, she couldn't untie it, so she rushed home to get her sewing basket. She took her scissors, and *snip! snip! snip!* she cut open the sack.

One, two, three, four, five, six! Out bounded her little kids.
Mother Goat told each of the kids to find a big stone. She filled the empty sack with them and neatly sewed it shut.

43

After a while, the wicked wolf woke up. He threw the sack over his shoulder and started off again.

"My, this sack is heavy," he said. "What plump little kids I have caught."

The wolf was very hungry by the time he had carried that heavy sack all the way home. He opened it up right away.

"What!" cried the wolf. "Stones?"

He was very angry, and very disappointed, and very very hungry. So he packed his things, went home to his mother for supper, and never came back again.

THE MUSICIANS OF BREMEN

Once upon a time, Donko Donkey decided to go to the town of Bremen. Once he was there, he hoped to become a town musician.

As he walked down the road, he met Davy Dog and stopped to chat.

"Where are you going?" asked Davy Dog.

"I am going to Bremen to become a town musician," Donko replied.

Davy then and there decided that he would like to do that, too.

So off they went together on the road to Bremen.

45

As they walked along, they sang a happy duet, braying and barking together.

Kitty Cat heard them and ran to meet them. "Where are you going?" she asked.

When Donko and Davy told her, she decided that she wanted to be a town musician, too.

So off they went singing a trio.

They had not gone far when they met Rocky Rooster. When he found out what the three musicians were going to do, he asked, "May I join you? I can sing, too, cock-a-doodle-doo."

They welcomed him, and so there were four musicians on their way to Bremen.

But the town of Bremen was far away.
The dark night came, and they lost their way. They were tired from their long walk, and very hungry.

Then, off in the distance, they saw a light shining in the window of a house.

"Perhaps there we will find something to eat and a place to sleep," said Donko. "But we must first make sure that the people are friendly."

So they crept silently up to the house. Donko, who was the tallest, peeked in the window.

"What do you see?" asked Kitty Cat.

"Why, I see four robbers!" exclaimed Donko. "They are sitting around a table enjoying a great feast. And lying around the room are all kinds of things that they have stolen."

"We must think of a plan to chase the robbers away," said Davy.

The musicians were all very hungry and wanted to enjoy that feast themselves. The food didn't belong to the robbers anyway, for they had stolen it. So the four musicians thought of a plan.

Davy jumped up on Donko's back.
Kitty climbed up on Davy's back.
Rocky perched on Kitty's back.
Then Rocky began to crow,
Kitty began to meow,
Davy began to bark,
and Donko began to bray.

You never heard such an awful racket in all your life!

49

The robbers jumped up out of their
chairs in terror! They thought some
monster was about to eat them.
Out the door and into the forest they
ran, as fast as they could go.

The four musicians went in and
finished eating the robbers' supper.
My, but it tasted good!

Then they turned off the lights
and lay down for a good night's sleep.

Meanwhile, about midnight, the robbers
saw that the house was dark and quiet.
"We should not have been scared so
easily," said Grumbuff, the chief robber.
"One of us must sneak back in to see if it
is safe for us to return."
Grumbuff was too scared to go himself,
so he told Snaggle-Tooth Louie to go.

Trembling with fear, Snaggle-Tooth Louie entered the pitch-dark house.

He was fumbling about trying to light a candle when he tripped over Kitty Cat and woke her up. Kitty leaped up and scratched him.

Scared out of his wits, Snaggle-Tooth Louie ran to the door, where Davy bit him in the leg and Donko gave him a kick.

Rocky woke up and started crowing— "Cock-a-doodle-doo!"

52

Snaggle-Tooth Louie ran back to his gang in the forest.

"We must flee!" he cried. "There is a terrible gang of horrible creatures in the house! A witch flew up and scratched me. An ogre stabbed me with a knife.

A giant hit me with a club, and all the time someone was screeching, 'Kill the robber, do!'"

The four robbers quickly turned and ran away. They never went near that house again.

The four musicians were so pleased with the house, they decided to stay there.

And should you ever go by that way, you will probably hear sweet songs coming from the window as the four friends sing their merry tunes.

THE THREE BILLY GOATS GRUFF

Once upon a time, there were three Billy Goats Gruff.
One day, they wanted to eat some berries that grew on
a hill across the river from where they lived. To get to
the hill, they had to cross over a bridge.
But under this bridge lived a big, bad troll.

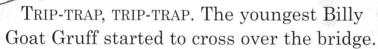

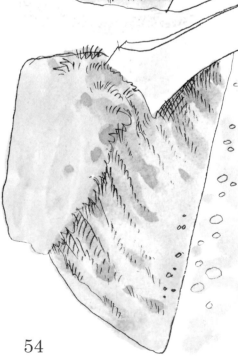

TRIP-TRAP, TRIP-TRAP. The youngest Billy
Goat Gruff started to cross over the bridge.
"Who trips over my bridge?" roared
the troll.
"Only Littlest Billy Goat Gruff," said
the little goat.
"Aha! I am coming up to eat you,"
said the troll.
"Oh, don't eat me," cried Littlest Billy
Goat Gruff. "My brother is coming after
me, and he is much bigger."
So the troll let the Littlest Billy Goat
Gruff cross the bridge.

54

Soon, TRIP-TRAP, TRIP-TRAP. The second
Billy Goat Gruff started to cross the bridge.
"Who trips over my bridge?" roared the troll.

"Only the Middle-Sized Billy Goat Gruff,"
said the second goat.
"Aha! I am coming up to eat you," said the troll.
"Oh, don't eat me," cried Middle-Sized
Billy Goat Gruff. "My brother is coming
after me, and he is much bigger."
So the troll let Middle-Sized Billy
Goat Gruff cross the bridge.

Soon, TRIP-TRAP, TRIP-TRAP. The biggest
Billy Goat Gruff started to cross the bridge.
"Who trips over my bridge?" roared the troll.
"It is I, Great Big Billy Goat Gruff," said the biggest goat.
"Aha! I am coming up to eat you," said the troll.
"Come along, then," said Great Big Billy Goat Gruff.
So up came the old troll.

Well! Great Big Billy Goat Gruff put down
his head and butted that ugly troll right
off the bridge, and he was never seen again.

Then the three Billy Goats Gruff ate
those delicious berries until they grew so
round and plump, they were scarcely able
to walk home again.

THE THREE WISHES

Once upon a time, there was a poor woodcutter who lived with his wife in a humble cottage.

One day, he said to himself, "I work hard all day, but I never earn enough money to buy all the things that we want."

A beautiful fairy overheard him.

She said to the woodcutter, "I will grant you three wishes, but choose them carefully, as you may have no more than three."

Then, in a wink, she disappeared.

The woodcutter hurried home to tell his wife about their three wishes.

She was very happy as she thought about all the things she would like to have.

There were so many things they wanted, they couldn't decide what to wish for.

"Let us think about it some more before we wish," said the woodcutter as he sat down to a bowl of soup for supper.

"Oh dear," he said. "How I wish I could have a nice fat sausage for a change."

And just like that, there was a nice fat sausage in his dish.

His wife was furious.

"Look what you've done!" she shouted. "You have wasted a wish on a foolish old sausage. How could you be so stupid? Now we only have two wishes left."

She kept on complaining until the woodcutter became so sick of hearing about the sausage that he shouted without thinking, "Oh, I wish that the sausage was stuck on the end of your nose!"

And lo and behold, the sausage jumped to the end of her nose and stuck fast.

"Now look what you've done!" she cried. "You've wasted another wish. Get this sausage off my nose!"

They tried to pull the sausage off, but it would not come unstuck.

"Well, we still have one wish left," said the woodcutter. "Let's think about what to wish for."

"What's there to think about?" cried his wife. "I can't go around with this sausage hanging from my nose. I wish this sausage would go away."

In a wink, the sausage disappeared. And so after their three wishes, the woodcutter and his wife were no better off than before. They didn't even get to eat the sausage for supper. Dear oh dear!

THE TEENY-TINY WOMAN

Once upon a time, there was a teeny-tiny
woman who lived in a teeny-tiny house.

One teeny-tiny day, the teeny-tiny woman
put on her teeny-tiny shawl and went out of
her teeny-tiny house for a teeny-tiny walk.

She walked for a teeny-tiny time until
she came to a teeny-tiny church. She
opened the teeny-tiny gate to the teeny-
tiny churchyard and went in.

Inside the teeny-tiny churchyard, the teeny-tiny woman found a teeny-tiny bone.

The teeny-tiny woman said to her teeny-tiny self, "This teeny-tiny bone will make some good teeny-tiny soup for my teeny-tiny supper."

So she put the teeny-tiny bone in her teeny-tiny pocket and went back to her teeny-tiny house. She went up her teeny-tiny stairs to her teeny-tiny bedroom.

She put the teeny-tiny bone in her teeny-tiny cupboard and closed the teeny-tiny doors.

Then, as she was a teeny-tiny bit tired, she got into her teeny-tiny bed to have a teeny-tiny nap.

She was asleep only a teeny-tiny time when she was awakened by a teeny-tiny voice from the teeny-tiny cupboard saying, "Give me my bone!"

61

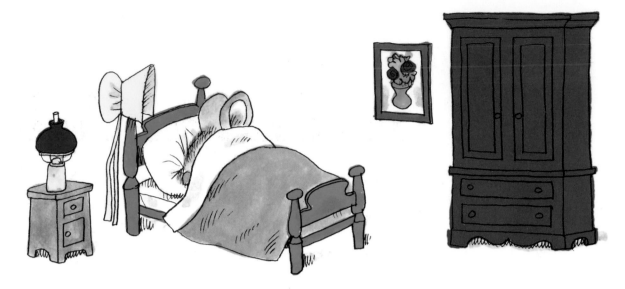

The teeny-tiny woman was a teeny-tiny bit frightened, so she hid her teeny-tiny head under the teeny-tiny covers and went to sleep again.

A teeny-tiny bit later, the teeny-tiny voice cried out, a teeny-tiny bit louder, "GIVE ME MY BONE!"

This made the teeny-tiny woman a teeny-tiny bit more frightened, and she hid her teeny-tiny head a teeny-tiny bit more under the teeny-tiny covers.

The teeny-tiny woman was asleep again for a teeny-tiny time when the teeny-tiny voice from the teeny-tiny cupboard called out a teeny-tiny bit louder,

"GIVE ME MY BONE!"

The teeny-tiny woman was even a teeny-tiny bit more frightened, but she stuck her teeny-tiny head out from under the teeny-tiny covers and said in her loudest teeny-tiny voice,

"TAKE IT!"

And that is the teeny-tiny end of this teeny-tiny story.

FIVE LITTLE PIGS

This little pig went to market.

This little pig stayed at home.

This little pig had roast beef.

This little pig had none.

And this little pig cried,
"Wee, wee, wee, I can't find my way home!"

63

THE LITTLE RED HEN

Once upon a time, a Pig, a Cat, a Duck, and a Little Red Hen lived together in a little house. The Pig, the Cat, and the Duck were all very lazy and would never help with the work around the house.

So the Little Red Hen had to do everything all by herself.

One day, as the Little Red Hen was raking in the yard, she found some seeds.
"Who will help me plant these grains of wheat?" she asked.

"Not I," said the Pig.

"Not I," said the Cat.

"Not I," said the Duck.

"Then I will do it myself," said the Little Red Hen. And she did.

65

Soon the wheat grew tall and golden.
"Who will help me cut the wheat?" asked
the Little Red Hen.

"Not I," said the Pig.

"Not I," said the Cat.

"Not I," said the Duck.

"Then I will do it myself,"
said the Little Red Hen.
And she did.

When the grain
was cut and ready to
be ground into flour,
the Little Red Hen
asked, "Who will
help me take the
grain to the mill?"

"Not I," said the Pig.

"Not I," said the Duck.

"Not I," said the Cat.

"Then I will do it myself,"
said the Little Red Hen.
And she did.

When the flour came back from the mill,
the Little Red Hen asked, "Who will help
me make this flour into bread?"
"Not I," said the Pig.
"Not I," said the Cat.
"Not I," said the Duck.

"Then I will do it myself,"
said the Little Red Hen.
And she did.
She made the flour into dough.
She rolled the dough into a loaf,
and she put it into the oven to bake.

When the loaf was baked, she took
it out of the oven.
Mmmmmm! Didn't it smell good!

"Who will help me eat this bread?"
asked the Little Red Hen.
"I will," said the Pig.
"I will," said the Cat.
"I will," said the Duck.

"Oh no, you won't!" said the Little Red Hen.
"I found the seed. I planted it. I harvested it.
I took the grain to the mill. I made the flour into bread.
And none of you would help me. I did the work all by
myself, and now I am going to eat the bread all by myself."
And she did.